The Worst Witch

Jill Murphy started putting books together (literally with a stapler) when she was six. Her Worst Witch series, the first book of which was published in 1974, is hugely successful. She has also written and illustrated several award-winning picture books for younger children.

Books by Jill Murphy

THE WORST WITCH

THE WORST WITCH STRIKES AGAIN

A BAD SPELL FOR THE WORST WITCH

THE WORST WITCH ALL AT SEA

THE WORST WITCH SAVES THE DAY

THE WORST WITCH TO THE RESCUE

THE WORST WITCH AND THE WISHING STAR

DEAR HOUND

THE WORST WITCH

JILL MURPHY

PUFFIN

PUFFIN BOOKS

UK | USA | Canada | Ireland | Australia
India | New Zealand | South Africa

Puffin Books is part of the Penguin Random House group of companies
whose addresses can be found at global.penguinrandomhouse.com.

www.penguin.co.uk
www.puffin.co.uk
www.ladybird.co.uk

First published by Alison & Busby 1974
Published by Puffin Books 1978
This edition published 2017

001

Copyright © Jill Murphy, 1974

The moral right of the author/illustrator has been asserted

Typeset in Baskerville
Printed in Great Britain by Clays Ltd, St Ives plc

A CIP catalogue record for this book is available from the British Library

ISBN: 978–0–141–38607–2

All correspondence to:
Puffin Books
Penguin Random House Children's
80 Strand, London WC2R ORL

This book belongs
to

For Reeeney

CHAPTER ONE

MISS CACKLE'S Academy for Witches stood at the top of a high mountain surrounded by a pine forest. It looked more like a prison than a school, with its gloomy grey walls and turrets. Sometimes you could see the pupils on their broomsticks flitting like bats above the playground wall, but usually the place was half hidden in mist, so that if you had glanced up at the mountain you would probably not have noticed the building was there at all.

Everything about the school was dark and shadowy. There were long, narrow corridors and winding staircases – and of course there were the girls themselves, dressed in black gymslips, black stockings, black hob-nailed boots, grey shirts and black-and-grey ties. Even their summer dresses were black-and-grey checked. The only touches of colour were the sashes round their gymslips – a different colour for each house – and the school badge, which was a black cat sitting on a yellow moon. For special occasions, such a prize-giving or Hallowe'en, there was another uniform consisting of a long robe worn with a tall, pointed hat, but as these were black too, it didn't really make much of a change.

There were so many rules that you couldn't do *any*thing without being told off, and there seemed to be tests and exams every week.

Mildred Hubble was in her first year at the school. She was one of those people who always seem to be in trouble. She didn't exactly mean to break rules and

annoy the teachers, but things just seemed
to *happen* whenever she was around. You
could rely on Mildred to have her hat on
back-to-front or her bootlaces trailing
along the floor. She couldn't walk from
one end of a corridor to the other without
someone yelling at her, and nearly every
night she was writing lines or being kept in
(not that there was anywhere to go if you
were allowed out). Anyway, she had lots
of friends, even if they did keep their
distance in the potion laboratory, and her
best friend Maud stayed loyally by
her through everything, however hair-
raising. They made a funny pair, for
Mildred was tall and thin with long plaits
which she often chewed absent-mindedly
(another thing she was told off about),
while Maud was short and tubby, had
round glasses and wore her hair in
bunches.

   On her first day at the academy each

pupil was given a broomstick and taught to ride it, which takes quite a long time and isn't nearly as easy as it looks. Halfway through the first term they were each presented with a black kitten which they trained to ride the broomsticks. The cats weren't for any practical purpose except to keep tradition going; some schools present owls instead, but it's just a matter of taste. Miss Cackle was a very traditional headmistress who did not believe in any new-fangled nonsense and trained her young witches to keep up all the customs that had been taught in her young day. At the end of the first year, each pupil received a copy of *The Popular Book of Spells*, a three-inch-thick volume bound in black leather. This was not really to be used, as they already had paperback editions for the classroom, but like the cats it was another piece of tradition. Apart from yearly prize-giving, there were no more presentations until the fifth and final year when most pupils were awarded the Witches' Higher Certificate. It did not seem likely that Mildred would ever get that far. After only two days at the school she crashed her broomstick into the yard wall, breaking the broomstick in half and bending her hat. She mended the stick with glue and sticky-tape, and fortunately it still flew, though there was an ugly bundle where the ends joined and sometimes it was rather difficult to control.

This story really begins halfway

through Mildred's first term, on the night before the presentation of the kittens ...

It was almost midnight and the school was in darkness except for one narrow window lit softly by the glow of a candle. This was Mildred's room where she was sitting in bed, wearing a pair of black-and-grey striped pyjamas and dropping off to sleep every few minutes. Maud was curled up on the end of the bed enveloped in a grey flannel nightdress and a black woollen shawl. Each pupil had the same type of room: very simple, with a wardrobe, iron bedstead, table and chair, and a slit window like the ones used by archers in castles of long ago. There was a picture-rail along the bare walls from which hung a sampler embroidered with a quotation from the *Book of Spells* and also, during the day, several bats. Mildred had three bats in her room, little furry ones which were very friendly. She was fond of animals and was looking forward to the next day when she would have a kitten of her own. Everyone was very excited about the presentation, and they had all spent the evening ironing their best robes and pushing the dents out of their best hats. Maud was too excited to sleep, so had sneaked into Mildred's room to talk about it with her friend.

'What are you going to call yours, Maud?' asked Mildred, sleepily.

'Midnight,' said Maud. 'I think it sounds dramatic.'

'I'm worried about the whole thing,' Mildred confessed, chewing the end of her plait. 'I'm sure I'll do something dreadful like treading on its tail, or else it'll take one look at me and leap out of the window. *Some*thing's bound to go wrong.'

'Don't be silly,' said Maud. 'You know you have a way with animals. And as for treading on its tail, it won't even be on the floor. Miss Cackle hands it to you, and that's all there is to it. So there's nothing to worry about, is there?'

Before Mildred had time to reply, the door crashed open to reveal their form-mistress, Miss Hardbroom, standing in the doorway wrapped in a black dressing-gown, with a lantern in her hand. She was a tall, terrifying lady with a sharp, bony face and black hair scragged back into such a tight knot that her forehead looked quite stretched.

'Rather late to be up, isn't it, girls?' she inquired nastily.

The girls, who had leapt into each other's arms when the door burst open, drew apart and fixed their eyes on the floor.

'Of course, if we don't want to be included in the presentation tomorrow we are certainly going about it the right way,' Miss Hardbroom continued icily.

'Yes, Miss Hardbroom,' chorused the girls miserably.

Miss Hardbroom glared meaningfully at Mildred's candle and swept out into the corridor with Maud in front of her.

Mildred hastily blew out the candle and dived under the bedclothes, but she could not get to sleep. Outside the window

she could hear the owls hooting, and somewhere in the school a door had been left open and was creaking backwards and forwards in the wind. To tell you the truth, Mildred was afraid of the dark, but don't tell anyone. I mean, whoever heard of a *witch* who was scared of the dark?

CHAPTER TWO

THE presentation took place in the Great Hall, a huge stone room with rows of wooden benches, a raised platform at one end and shields and portraits all round the walls. The whole school had assembled, and Miss Cackle and Miss Hardbroom stood behind a table on the platform. On the table was a large wicker basket from which came mews and squeaks.

First of all everyone sang the school song, which went like this:

Onward, ever striving onward,
Proudly on our brooms we fly
Straight and true above the treetops,
Shadows on the moonlit sky.

Ne'er a day will pass before us
When we have not tried our best,
Kept our cauldrons bubbling nicely,
Cast our spells and charms with zest.

Full of joy we mix our potions,
Working by each other's side.
When our days at school are over
Let us think of them with pride.

It was the usual type of school song, full

of pride, joy and striving. Mildred had never yet mixed a potion with joy, nor flown her broomstick with pride – she was usually too busy trying to keep upright!

Anyway, when they had finished droning the last verse, Miss Cackle rang the little silver bell on her table and the girls marched up in single file to receive their kittens. Mildred was the last of all, and when she reached the table Miss Cackle pulled out of the basket not a sleek black kitten like all the others but a little tabby with white paws and the sort of fur that looked as if it had been out all night in a gale.

'We ran out of black ones,' explained Miss Cackle with a pleasant grin.

Miss Hardbroom smiled too, but nastily.

After the ceremony everyone rushed to see Mildred's kitten.

'I think H.B. had a hand in this somewhere,' said Maud darkly. ('H.B.' was their nickname for Miss Hardbroom.)

'I must admit, it does look a bit dim, doesn't it?' said Mildred, scratching the tabby kitten's head. 'But I don't really mind. I'll just have to think of another name – I was going to call it Sooty. Let's take them down to the playground and see what they make of broomstick riding.'

Almost all the first-year witches were in the yard trying to persuade their puzzled kittens to sit on their broomsticks. Several were already clinging on by their claws, and one kitten, belonging to a rather smug young witch named Ethel, was sitting bolt upright cleaning its paws, as if it had been broomstick riding all its life!

Riding a broomstick was no easy matter, as I have mentioned before. First, you ordered the stick to hover, and it hovered lengthways above the ground. Then you sat on it, gave it a sharp tap, and away you flew. Once in the air you could make the stick do almost anything by saying, 'Right! Left! Stop! Down a bit!' and so on. The difficult part was balancing, for if you leaned a little too far to one side you could easily overbalance, in which case you would either fall off or find yourself hanging upside-down and then you would just have to hold on with your skirt over your head until a friend came to your rescue.

It had taken Mildred several weeks of falling off and crashing before she could ride the broomstick reasonably well, and it looked as though her kitten was going to have the same trouble. When she put it on the end of the stick, it just fell off without even trying to hold on. After many attempts, Mildred picked up her kitten and gave it a shake.

'Listen!' she said severely. 'I think I shall have to call you Stupid. You don't even *try* to hold on. Everyone else is all right – look at all your friends.'

The kitten gazed at her sadly and licked her nose with its rough tongue.

'Oh, come on,' said Mildred, softening her voice. 'I'm not really angry with you. Let's try again.'

And she put the kitten back on the broomstick, from which it fell with a thud.

Maud was having better luck. Her kitten was hanging on grimly upside down.

'Oh, well,' laughed Maud. 'It's a start.'

'Mine's useless,' said Mildred, sitting on the broomstick for a rest.

'Never mind,' Maud said. 'Think how

hard it must be for them to hang on by their claws.'

An idea flashed into Mildred's head, and she dived into the school, leaving her kitten chasing a leaf along the ground and the broomstick still patiently hovering. She came out carrying her satchel which she hooked over the end of the broom and then bundled the kitten into it. The kitten's astounded face peeped out of the bag as Mildred flew delightedly round the yard.

'Look, Maud!' she called from ten feet up in the air.

'That's cheating!' said Maud, looking at the satchel.

Mildred flew back and landed on the ground laughing.

'I don't think H.B. will approve,' said Maud doubtfully.

'Quite right, Maud,' an icy voice behind them said. 'Mildred, my dear, possibly it would be even easier with handlebars and a saddle.'

Mildred blushed.

'I'm sorry, Miss Hardbroom,' she muttered. 'It doesn't balance very well – my kitten, so … I thought … perhaps …' Her voice trailed away under Miss Hardbroom's stony glare and Mildred unhooked her satchel and turned the bewildered kitten on to the ground.

'Girls!' Miss Hardbroom clapped her hands. 'I would remind you that there is a potion test tomorrow morning. That is all.'

So saying, she disappeared – literally.

'I wish she wouldn't do that,' whispered Maud, looking at the place where their form-mistress had been standing. 'You're never quite sure whether she's gone or not.'

'Right again, Maud,' came Miss Hardbroom's voice from nowhere.

Maud gulped and hurried back to her kitten.

CHAPTER THREE

DO you remember I told you about a certain young witch named Ethel who had succeeded in teaching her kitten from the very first try? Ethel was one of those lucky people for whom everything goes right. She was always top of the class, her spells always worked, and Miss Hardbroom never made any icy remarks to her. Because of this, Ethel was often rather bossy with the other girls.

On this occasion she had overheard the whole of Mildred's encounter with Miss Hardbroom and couldn't resist being nasty about it.

'I think Miss Cackle gave you that cat on purpose,' Ethel sneered. 'You're both as bad as each other.'

'Oh, be quiet,' said Mildred, trying to keep her temper. 'Anyway, it's not a bad cat. It'll learn in time.'

'Like you did?' Ethel went on. 'Wasn't it last week that you crashed into the dustbins?'

'*Look*, Ethel,' Mildred said, 'you'd better be quiet, because if you don't I shall . . .'

'Well?'

'I shall have to turn you into a frog – and I don't want to do that.'

Ethel gave a shriek of laughter.

'That's really funny!' she crowed. 'You don't even know the beginners' spells, let alone ones like that.'

Mildred blushed and looked very miserable.

'Go on, then!' cried Ethel. 'Go *on*, then,

if you're so clever. *Turn* me into a frog!
I'm waiting.'

It just so happened that Mildred did
have an idea of that spell (she had been
reading about it in the library). By now,
everyone had crowded round, waiting to
see what would happen, and Ethel was
still jeering. It was unbearable.

Mildred muttered the spell under her
breath – and Ethel vanished. In her place
stood a small pink and grey pig.

Cries and shouts rent the air:

'Oh, no!'

'That's torn it!'

'You've done it now, Mildred!'

Mildred was horrified. 'Oh, Ethel,' she
said. 'I'm sorry, but you did ask for it.'

The pig looked furious.

'You *beast*, Mildred Hubble!' it
grunted. 'Change me back!'

At that moment Miss Hardbroom suddenly appeared in the middle of the yard.

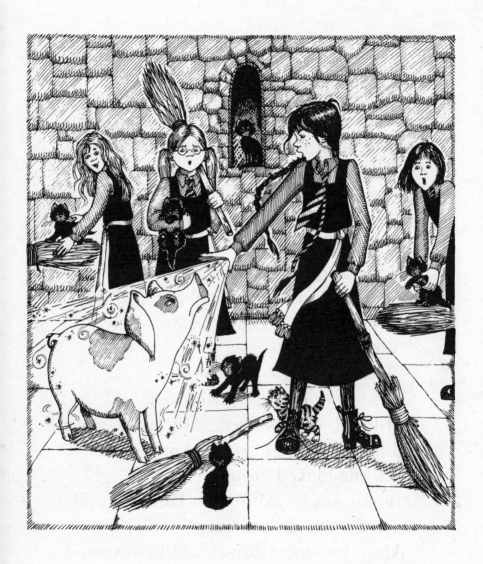

'Where is Ethel Hallow?' she asked.
'Miss Bat would like to see her about extra
chanting lessons.'

Her sharp gaze fell on the small pig
which was grunting softly at her feet.

'What is this animal doing in the yard?'
she asked, coldly.

Everyone looked at Mildred.

'I ... let it in, Miss Hardbroom,'
Mildred said hesitantly.

'Well, you can just let it out again,
please,' said Miss Hardbroom.

'Oh, I can't do that!' gasped the
unhappy Mildred. 'I mean, well ... er ...
Couldn't I keep it as a pet?'

'I think you have quite enough trouble
coping with yourself and that kitten without adding a pig to your worries,' replied
Miss Hardbroom, staring at the tabby
kitten which was peering round Mildred's
ankles. 'Let it out at once! Now, where is
Ethel?'

Mildred bent down.

'Ethel, dear,' she whispered coaxingly in the pig's ear. 'Will you go out when I tell you to? Please, Ethel, I'll let you in again straight away afterwards.'

Pleading with people like Ethel never works. It only makes them feel their power.

'I *won't* go!' bellowed the pig. 'Miss Hardbroom, I *am* Ethel! Mildred Hubble turned me into a pig.'

Nothing ever surprised Miss Hardbroom. Even this startling piece of news only caused her to raise one slanting eyebrow.

'Well, Mildred,' she said, 'I am glad to know that you have at least learned *one* thing since you came here. However, as you will have noticed in the Witches' Code, rule number seven, paragraph two, it is not customary to practise such tricks on your fellows. Please remove the spell at once.'

'I'm afraid I don't know how to,' Mildred confessed, in a very small voice.

Miss Hardbroom stared at her for a few moments.

'Then you had better go and look it up in the library,' she said, wearily. 'Take Ethel with you, and on your way drop in and tell Miss Bat why Ethel will be late.'

Mildred picked up her kitten and hurried inside, followed by the pig. Fortunately, Miss Bat was not in her room, but it was most embarrassing going into the library. Ethel was grunting loudly on purpose and everyone stared so much that Mildred could have crawled under the table.

'Hurry up,' moaned the pig.

'Oh, stop going on!' said Mildred, as she flicked hastily through the huge spell book. 'It's all your fault, anyway. You actually *asked* me to do it. I don't see why you're complaining.'

'I said a frog, not a pig,' said Ethel, pettily. 'You couldn't even do *that* right.'

Mildred ignored the grunting Ethel and kept looking in the book. It took her half an hour to find the right spell, and soon after that Ethel was her horrible self again. The people in the library were most surprised to see the pig suddenly change into a furious-looking Ethel.

'Now, don't be angry, Ethel,' Mildred said softly. 'Remember: "Silence in the library at all times".'

And she rushed into the corridor.

'Wasn't that awful, Cat?' she said to the kitten, which was curled up inside her cardigan. 'I think I'd better put you in my room and then go and revise for the potion test. Don't tease the bats, will you?'

CHAPTER FOUR

IT was the morning of the potion test, and the girls were filing into the potion lab, each hoping she had learned the right spell, except for Ethel who knew everything and never worried about such matters.

'Come along, girls! Two to a cauldron!' barked Miss Hardbroom. 'Today we shall make a laughter potion. No textbooks to be used – put that book away this *instant*, Mildred! Work quietly, and when you have finished you may take a small sip of the mixture to make sure it is correctly made. You may begin.'

Maud and Mildred were sharing a cauldron, of course, but unfortunately neither of them had learned that particular spell.

'I think I can remember it vaguely,' whispered Maud. 'Bits of it, anyway.' She began to sort through the ingredients which had been laid out on each workbench.

When everything was stirred together in the cauldron, the bubbling liquid was bright pink. Mildred stared at it doubtfully.

'I'm sure it should be green,' she said. 'In fact I'm sure we should have put in a handful of pondweed-gathered-at-midnight.'

'Are you *sure*?' asked Maud.

'Yes ...,' replied Mildred, not very definitely.

'*Absolutely* sure?' Maud asked again.

'You know what happened last time.'

'I'm *quite* sure,' insisted Mildred. 'Anyway, there's a handful of pondweed laid out on each bench. I'm positive we're supposed to put it in.'

'Oh, all right,' said Maud. 'Go on, then. It can't do any harm.'

Mildred grabbed the pondweed and dropped it into the mixture. They took turns at stirring it for a few minutes until it began to turn dark green.

'What a horrid colour,' said Maud.

'Are you ready, girls?' asked Miss Hardbroom, rapping on her desk. 'You should have been ready minutes ago. A laughter potion should be made quickly for use in an emergency.'

Ethel was still working on the bench in front of Mildred, who stood on tiptoe to sneak a look at the colour of Ethel's potion. To her horror, it was bright pink.

'Oh, no,' Mildred thought, with a

sinking feeling. 'I wonder what potion we've made?'

Miss Hardbroom banged on the desk again.

'We shall now test the potion,' she commanded. 'Not too much, please. We don't want anyone hysterical.'

Each pupil took a test-tubeful of liquid and drank a little. At once shrieks of laughter rang through the room, especially from Ethel's bench where they had made the best potion of all and were laughing so much that tears rolled down their cheeks. The only two girls who weren't laughing were Mildred and Maud.

'Oh, dear,' said Maud. 'I feel most peculiar. Why aren't we laughing, Mil?'

'I hate to tell you,' confessed Mildred, 'I think –' But before she had time to say any more, the two girls had disappeared!

'Cauldron number two!' snapped Miss

Hardbroom. 'You seem to have made the wrong spell.'

'It was my fault,' said Mildred's voice from behind the cauldron.

'That I do not doubt,' Miss Hardbroom said sourly. 'You had both better sit down until you reappear, and then, Mildred, perhaps a trip to Miss Cackle's office would do you some good. You can explain why I sent you.'

Everyone had left the room by the time the two young witches finally began to reappear. This was a very slow process, with first the head and then the rest of the body becoming gradually visible.

'I'm sorry,' said Mildred's head and shoulders.

'That's all right,' said Maud's head. 'I just wish you'd *think* a bit more. We had the right potion to start with.'

'Sorry,' mumbled Mildred again, then she began to laugh. 'Hey, Maud, you do

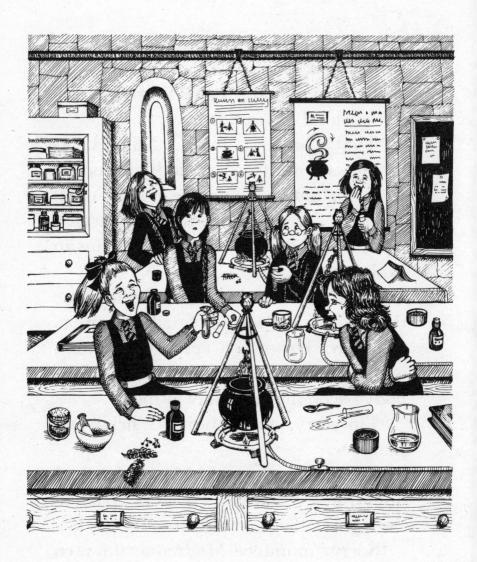

look funny with just your head showing!'

At once they both began to laugh, and soon they were best friends again.

'I suppose I'd better go and see Old Cackle now,' said Mildred, when she had completely reappeared.

'I'll come with you to the door,' offered Maud.

Miss Cackle was small and very fat, with short grey hair and green horn-rimmed glasses which she usually wore pushed up on top of her head. She was the exact opposite of Miss Hardbroom, being absent-minded in appearance and rather gentle by nature. The girls were not in the least bit afraid of her, whereas Miss Hard-broom could reduce any of them to a miserable heap with just one word. Miss Cackle used a different technique. By always being friendly and pleased to see a pupil in her office, she made them feel embarrassed if they had something un-pleasant to tell her, as Mildred nearly always had.

Mildred knocked at Miss Cackle's door, hoping she would be out. She wasn't.

'Come in!' called the familiar voice from inside.

Mildred opened the door and went in. Miss Cackle, glasses on her nose for once, was busily writing in a huge register. She looked up and peered over her spectacles.

'Ah, Mildred,' she said pleasantly.

'Come and sit down while I finish filling in this register.'

Mildred closed the door and sat by Miss Cackle's desk.

'I wish she wasn't so pleased to see me,' she thought.

Miss Cackle slammed the register shut and pushed her glasses on to the top of her head.

'Now, Mildred, what can I do for you?'

Mildred twisted her fingers together.

'Well, actually, Miss Cackle,' she began slowly, 'Miss Hardbroom sent me to see you because I made the wrong potion again.'

The smile faded from the headmistress's face and she sighed, as if with deep disappointment. Mildred felt about an inch high.

'*Really*, Mildred,' Miss Cackle said in a tired voice, 'I have run out of things to say to you. Week after week you come here,

sent by every member of staff in the school, and my words just seem to go straight in one ear and out of the other. You will never get the Witches' Higher Certificate if this appalling conduct continues. You must be the worst witch in the entire school. Whenever there's any trouble you are nearly always to be found at the bottom of it, and it's just not good enough, my dear. Now, what have you to say for yourself *this* time?'

'I don't really know, Miss Cackle,' Mildred said humbly. 'Everything I do just seems to go wrong, that's all. I don't *mean* to do it.'

'Well, that's no excuse, is it?' said Miss Cackle. 'Everyone else manages to live without causing an uproar wherever they go. You must pull yourself together, Mildred. I don't want to hear *any* more bad reports about you, do you understand?'

'Yes, Miss Cackle,' said Mildred, in as sorry a voice as she could manage.

'Run along, then,' said the head-mistress, 'and remember what I have said to you.'

Maud was waiting in the corridor, eager to know what had been said, when her friend came out of the office.

'She's nice really,' Mildred said. 'Just told me all the usual things. She hates telling people off. I'll have to try to be better from now on. Come on, let's go and give the kittens another broomstick lesson.'

CHAPTER FIVE

THE following morning, Miss Hardbroom strode into the class-room looking thoughtful. She was wearing a new grey-and-black striped dress, with a brooch at the shoulder.

'Good morning, girls,' she greeted them, not as sharply as usual.

'Good morning, Miss Hardbroom,' chorused the girls.

Their form-mistress arranged the books on her desk and surveyed the class.

'I have something to tell you, girls,' she

began, 'that gives me great pleasure on one hand, yet causes me some worry on the other.' Here she shot a glance at Mildred. 'As you know, the Hallowe'en celebrations take place in two weeks' time and it is customary for a display to be presented by this school. This year, our class has been chosen to present the display.'

There were gasps of delight from the girls.

'Of course,' Miss Hardbroom went on, 'it is a great honour, but also a responsibility, as Miss Cackle's Academy has a very high reputation which we don't want to spoil, *do we*? Last year, Form Three produced a play which was highly praised, and I thought that this year we might present a broomstick formation team. You will need a lot of practice, as some of you are not too steady on your broomsticks yet, but I am quite certain that we could give an interesting and successful performance. Is there anyone who would prefer something different?'

She looked round piercingly at the girls, who all shrank into their seats and would not have dared to disagree, even if they had wanted to.

'Good,' said Miss Hardbroom. 'Then it is settled. We shall present a broomstick formation team. Let us go down to the yard and begin to practise at once. Fetch your broomsticks and be outside in two minutes.' With which words she vanished.

The girls excitedly clattered from the room and rushed along the corridors to fetch their broomsticks, which were kept in their own rooms. The spiral staircase rang with the sound of hob-nailed boots as the girls rushed down to the yard, where they found Miss Hardbroom waiting for them.

'First of all, you'd better take a practice flight,' she said. 'Form an orderly crocodile and go round the school and back.'

Off they all flew in an orderly, but rather wobbly, procession round the school.

'Quite good, girls,' said Miss Hardbroom, as they lined up in front of her. 'You were swaying about rather badly, Mildred, but apart from that, you all did quite well. Now, I have made out a list of the things you will be doing. First, a single line, with each pupil sinking and rising alternately. This should be comparatively easy. Secondly, a flying "V" similar to wild geese in flight. Then, nose-diving the yard, and swooping up just before you reach the ground. That will be the most difficult part of all.' Mildred and Maud exchanged horrified glances. 'And finally you will form a circle in the air, each broomstick touching the next. Any

questions? No? Very well, then, we shall
begin the first item immediately. What
was the first item, Mildred?'

'... er, nose-diving the yard, Miss
Hardbroom.'

'Wrong. Ethel, do you remember?'

'We are to form a line, each pupil
sinking and rising alternately,' replied
Ethel, word-perfect as always.

'Correct,' said Miss Hardbroom, with a
frosty glare at Mildred. 'We shall practise
all this morning and every morning until
the celebrations, and perhaps this after-

noon, if I can persuade Miss Bat to allow you to miss your chanting lesson.'

They worked very hard for the next two weeks. Every spare minute was spent practising and, by the time Hallowe'en arrived, the display was quite a joy to watch. Maud's hat was squashed like a concertina from the time when she had not pulled up from a nose-dive during practice, but apart from that there had been hardly any trouble at all, even from Mildred, who was making a special effort to be good and thoughtful.

The day before Hallowe'en, Miss Hard-broom lined up her class in the yard to give them a few final words of advice.

'I am very pleased with you, girls,' she said, almost pleasantly. 'Now, you will be wearing your best robes tomorrow, so I hope they will be clean and pressed.'

As she said this she caught sight of Mildred's broomstick.

'Mildred, why is there a bundle of sticky-tape in the middle of your broomstick?'

'I'm afraid I broke it in half during the first week of term,' admitted Mildred.

Ethel giggled.

'I see,' said Miss Hardbroom. 'Well, you certainly can't use that one in the display. Ethel, I seem to remember you have a spare one. Perhaps you could lend it to Mildred?'

'Oh, Miss Hardbroom!' cried Ethel. 'It was given to me as a birthday present. I shouldn't want anything to happen to it.'

Miss Hardbroom fixed Ethel with one of her nastiest looks.

'If that is how you feel, Ethel,' she said in icy tones, 'then –'

'Oh, I didn't mean I *won't* lend it, Miss Hardbroom,' Ethel said, meekly. 'I'll go and fetch it now.' And she ran into the school.

Ethel had never forgotten the time Mildred had turned her into a pig, and as she made her way up the spiral staircase she suddenly thought of a marvellous way of taking her revenge. (Ethel really wasn't a nice person at all.)

'I'll fix you, Mildred Hubble,' she cackled to herself, as she took the broomstick out of her cupboard. 'Now, listen to me, Broom, this is very important . . .'

The class had dismissed when Ethel returned carrying the broomstick. Mildred was practising nose-diving the yard.

'Here's the broom, Mildred,' called Ethel. 'I'll leave it propped against the wall.'

'Thanks very much,' replied Mildred, delighted that Ethel was being so nice, for the two hadn't spoken since the pig episode. 'It's very kind of you.'

'Not at all,' said Ethel, smiling wickedly to herself as she went back into the school.

CHAPTER SIX

HALLOWE'EN was celebrated each year in the ruins of an old castle quite near the school. The special fires were lit at sunset, and by dark all the witches and wizards had assembled.

As the sun set, the members of Miss Cackle's Academy were preparing to leave the school. Mildred smoothed her robes, said good-bye to her kitten, put on her hat, grabbed Ethel's broomstick and ran down to the yard. She took a quick look out of her window before leaving the room and saw the fires being lit in the distance. It was very exciting.

The rest of the school had already assembled as Mildred rushed out of the door and took her place. Miss Hardbroom looked splendid in her full witch's robes and hat.

'Everyone is present now,' Miss Hardbroom announced to Miss Cackle.

'Then we shall set off,' said the headmistress. 'To the celebrations! Class Five first, Class Four second, and so on until Class One!'

They made a wonderful sight flying

over the trees towards the castle, cloaks soaring in the wind, and the older girls with their cats perched on the ends of their broomsticks. Miss Hardbroom looked particularly impressive, sitting bolt-upright with her long black hair streaming behind her. The girls had never seen her hair loose before and were amazed how much of it she could possibly scrag into that tight knot every day. It came down to her waist.

'H.B. looks quite nice with her hair like

that,' whispered Maud to Mildred, who was riding next to her.

'Yes,' agreed Mildred, 'she doesn't seem half as frightening.'

Miss Hardbroom turned round and shot a piercing look at the two girls.

'No talking!' she snapped.

A huge crowd was already there at the castle when they arrived. The pupils of the Academy lined up in neat rows while Miss Cackle and all the other teachers shook hands with the chief wizard. He was very old, with a long white beard and a purple gown embroidered with moons and stars.

'And what have you prepared for us this year?' he asked.

'We have prepared a broomstick formation team, Your Honour,' Miss Cackle replied. 'Shall we begin, Miss Hardbroom?'

Miss Hardbroom clapped her hands

and the girls lined up, with Ethel at the front.

'You may begin,' said Miss Hard-broom.

Ethel rose perfectly into the air, followed by the rest of the class. First, they made a line, sinking and rising, which received great applause. Then they nose-dived the yard. (Miss Cackle closed her eyes during this part, but nothing went wrong.) Then the girls made a V in the air, which looked quite beautiful.

'Your girls get better every year,' remarked a young witch to Miss Hard-broom, who smiled.

Last of all came the circle, which was quite the easiest part.

'All over soon,' whispered Maud, arranging her broomstick in front of Mildred.

As soon as they had formed the circle, Mildred knew that something was the matter with her broomstick. It started to rock about, and seemed to be trying to throw her off balance.

'Maud!' she cried to her friend. 'There's something –' but before Mildred could say any more, the broomstick gave a violent kick like a bucking bronco and she fell off, grabbing at Maud as she fell.

There was chaos in the air. All the girls were screaming and clutching at each other, and soon there was a tangled mass of broomsticks and witches on the ground. The only girl who flew serenely back to earth was Ethel. A few of the younger witches laughed, but most of them looked grim.

'We are so sorry, Your Honour,' apologized Miss Cackle, as Miss Hard-broom untangled the heap of girls and jerked them to their feet. 'I'm sure there must be some simple explanation.'

'Miss Cackle,' said the chief magician,

sternly, 'your pupils are the witches of the future. I shudder to think what that future will be like.'

He paused, and there was complete silence. Miss Hardbroom glared at Mildred.

'However,' continued the chief magician, 'we shall forget this incident for the rest of the evening. Let us now begin the chanting.'

CHAPTER SEVEN

AT dawn the celebrations ended, and the pupils flew wearily back to school, some riding double as their own broomsticks were broken. No one was speaking to Mildred (even Maud was being very cool towards her friend), and Form One was in disgrace. When they arrived at the Academy, everyone was sent straight to bed. It was the custom, after the all-night Hallowe'en celebrations, to sleep until noon the next day.

'Mildred!' said Miss Cackle, in a sharp voice, as Form One made their way miserably up the stairs. 'Miss Hardbroom and I will see you in my office first thing tomorrow afternoon.'

'Yes, Miss Cackle,' replied Mildred, almost in tears, and she ran up the steps.

As Mildred opened her bedroom door, Ethel, who was behind her, leaned across and whispered, '*That*'ll teach you to go around changing people into pigs!' and she pulled a face and ran away down the corridor.

Mildred closed the door and fell on to her bed, almost flattening the kitten, which leapt out of the way just in time.

'Oh, Tabby,' she said, burying her face in the kitten's warm fur, 'I've had such a dreadful time, and it wasn't even my fault! I might have known Ethel wouldn't lend me her broomstick out of kindness.

Nobody will ever believe that it wasn't me just being clumsy as usual.'

The kitten licked her ear sympathetically, and the bats returned through the narrow window and settled upside down on the picture-rail.

Two hours later, Mildred was lying in bed, still wide awake. She was imagining what the interview with Miss Cackle and her terrible form-mistress would be like. The kitten was curled up peacefully on her chest.

'It'll be *aw*ful,' she thought, sadly looking towards the grey sky outside the window. 'I wonder if they'll expel me? Or perhaps I could tell them that it was Ethel – no, I would never do that. Suppose they decide to turn me into a frog? No, I'm sure they wouldn't do anything like that; Miss Hardbroom said that was against the Witches' Code. Oh, what *will* they do to me? Even Maud thinks it's my fault, and I've never seen H.B. look more furious.'

She lay thinking about it until she was really frightened, and suddenly she leapt out of bed.

'Come on, Tabby!' she said, pulling a bag out of the wardrobe. 'We're running away.'

She stuffed a few clothes and books into the bag and put on her best robe so that no one would recognize the usual school uniform. Then she picked up her broomstick, put the kitten into the bag, and crept out along the silent corridor to the spiral staircase.

'I shall miss the bats,' she thought.

It was a cold, dull morning, and Mildred pulled her cape about her shoulders as she crossed the yard, glancing round in case anyone was watching. The school seemed very strange with no one about. Mildred had to fly over the gates, which were locked as usual, but it was difficult to balance with the bag slung on the back of her broomstick, so she got off on the other side of the gates and started through the pine trees on foot.

'I don't know where we're going, Tabby,' she said, as they picked their way down the mountainside.

CHAPTER EIGHT

IT was very gloomy in the forest, and Mildred felt slightly uneasy, surrounded by dark trees which grew so thickly together that no light fell between them. When she was almost at the bottom of the mountain, she sat down to rest, leaning her back against a tree, and the kitten climbed out of the bag to stretch itself on the grass.

It was very quiet except for a few birds singing, and a rather strange noise, a sort of low humming, almost like a lot of people talking at once. In fact, the more Mildred listened, the more it did sound like voices. She looked in the direction of the noise and thought she saw something moving along the trees.

'Let's go and have a look, Tabby,' she whispered.

They left the bag and broomstick leaning against the tree, and crept through the tangled undergrowth. The noise grew louder.

'Why, it *is* people talking,' said Mildred. 'Look, Tabby, over there, through the branches.'

Sitting in a clearing in the gloom were about twenty witches, all crowded together, muttering and talking in low voices. Mildred crept nearer and listened. She didn't recognize any of them. A tall, grey-haired witch got to her feet.

'Listen, everyone,' said the grey-haired witch. 'Will you all be quiet for a few moments? Thank you. Now, what I should like to know is, are we quite sure that they will all be sleeping, or at least in their rooms?'

She sat down, and another witch got up to reply. She was a small, plump witch with green horn-rimmed glasses. For a horrible moment Mildred thought it was Miss Cackle, but her voice was different when she spoke.

'Of course we are sure,' this witch replied. 'The morning after Hallowe'en celebrations the entire school sleeps until midday. It is a rule, and the school is very strict about rules, so no one will be up until five minutes to twelve at the very earliest. If we fly over the wall into the back part of the yard, we will be as far away from the bedrooms as we can be, and no one will possibly hear us. Added to this, we shall all be invisible, so we shall be extremely well protected. Then all that remains to be done is to split up, sneak into each room and turn them all into frogs. They won't be able to see us even if they *are* awake. Remember to take one of these boxes with you for the frogs.' She pointed to a neat pile of small cardboard boxes. 'We can't have even one of them escaping. Once this is done, the entire school and everyone in it will be under our control.

'Is the invisibility potion ready yet?' she continued, turning to a young witch who was stirring a cauldron over a fire. It was the same potion that the two Ms had made during the laughter potion test.

'Another few minutes,' replied the young witch, dropping a handful of bats' whiskers into the mixture. 'It needs to simmer for a bit.'

Mildred was horrified. She sneaked back to where she had left her bag, and then into the shadows so that she couldn't be seen.

'What on earth can we do, Tab?' she

whispered to the kitten, imagining Maud hopping about turned into a frog. 'We can't let them take over the school.'

She rummaged through the bag and took out the two books she had brought with her. One was the Witches' Code and the other was her spell book. Mildred flicked through the spell book and stopped at the page about turning people into animals. There was only one example given, and that was snails.

'Dare I?' thought Mildred. 'Dare I turn the whole lot of them into snails?' The kitten looked at her, encouragingly.

'I know it's against the Witches' Code, Tabby,' she said, 'but *they* don't seem to follow any rules. They were planning to change us into frogs while we were *asleep*, so I don't see why we shouldn't do the same to them in self-defence.'

She sneaked back to the clearing, clutching her spell book.

'Here goes!' she thought desperately.

The invisibility potion was being poured out into cups, so Mildred had to work quickly. She waved her arms in a circle towards the crowd of witches (this part of spell-making can be very awkward when you don't want to draw attention to yourself) and muttered the spell under her breath. For a second, nothing happened, and the witches milling round the cauldron continued to chatter and bustle about. Mildred closed her eyes in despair, but when she opened them again everyone had vanished and on the ground was a group of snails of all different shapes and sizes.

'Tabby!' shrieked Mildred. 'I've done it! Look!'

Tabby came bounding out of the undergrowth and stared at the snails, who were all moving away as fast as they could, which wasn't very fast. Mildred took one of the cardboard boxes and put the snails into it, gently picking them up one by one.

'I suppose we'll have to take them back to school and tell Miss Cackle, Tab,' she said, suddenly remembering her interview to come at noon. 'Still, we'll have to go back. We can't just leave this lot here, can we?'

So they set off up the mountainside, Mildred carrying the box in her arms,

while the broomstick flew alongside with
the bag hanging from it and Tabby riding
inside the bag.

CHAPTER NINE

THE school was still completely deserted when Mildred arrived once more at the heavy iron gates. She hurried up the spiral staircase to her room and unpacked her bag so that no one would know she had tried to run away. Just as she was making her way to the door with the box in her arms, the door opened and Miss Hardbroom appeared.

'Would you kindly tell me what you are doing, Mildred?' she asked frostily. 'I have just watched you creeping up the corridor, complete with broomstick, cat, a bag and this cardboard box. Is it too much to ask for an explanation?'

'Oh, no, Miss Hardbroom,' replied Mildred, holding up the box for her form-mistress to see the contents. 'You see, I found a crowd of witches on the mountain-side, and they were planning to take over the school and change you all into frogs, and they were making an invisibility potion so you wouldn't be able to see them, so I turned them all into snails and brought . . .'

Her words trailed into silence as she saw the expression on Miss Hardbroom's face. Obviously, her form-mistress didn't believe a word.

'I suppose these are the witches?' she asked bitterly, pointing to the snails which were all huddled up in one corner of the box.

'Yes, they are!' Mildred insisted desperately. 'I know it sounds a peculiar story, Miss Hardbroom, but you must believe me. Their broomsticks and cauldrons and things are still in the clearing where I found them, really.'

'Well, you had better show the creatures to Miss Cackle,' said Miss Hardbroom, nastily. 'Go and wait in Miss Cackle's office while I fetch her – and I hope this isn't any sort of joke, Mildred. I seem to remember that you are already in a considerable amount of trouble.'

Mildred was perched nervously on the edge of a chair in the headmistress's office when Miss Hardbroom returned with Miss Cackle, who was wearing a grey dressing-gown, and looked half asleep.

'*These* are they,' stated Miss Hardbroom, pointing to the box on the desk.

Miss Cackle sat down heavily in her chair and looked first into the box and then at Mildred.

'Mildred,' she said in dramatic tones, 'I am still suffering from my public humiliation last night. Because of you the reputation of this school now lies in the mud, and yet you expect me to believe an incredible story like this?'

'But it's *true*!' cried Mildred. 'I can even describe some of them. One was tall and thin with thick grey hair, and there was another who looked just like you, Miss Cackle, if you'll excuse me being personal.

She had green horn-rimmed glasses –'

'Wait a moment!' said Miss Cackle, pushing her own glasses on to her nose. 'Did you say she had horn-rimmed glasses and looked like me?'

'Yes, Miss Cackle,' replied Mildred, blushing. 'Green ones. I'm sorry if you thought I was being rude.'

'No, no, child, it isn't that,' said Miss Cackle, peering into the box again. Then she turned to Miss Hardbroom. 'Do you know, I think the girl may be right after all. The person whom she described sounds exactly like my wicked sister Agatha who has always been extremely jealous of my position at this Academy!'

Miss Cackle stared over her glasses at the snails.

'Well, well, Agatha,' she chuckled. 'So we meet again. I wonder which of these beauties you are? What shall we do with them, Miss Hardbroom?'

'I suggest we change them back to their natural form again.'

'But we can't!' cried Miss Cackle in dismay. 'There are *twenty* of them.'

Miss Hardbroom looked faintly amused.

'May I point out,' she said, 'paragraph five of rule number seven in the Witches' Code, which states that anyone having been changed into any type of animal by another witch, for purposes of self-defence, cannot, on being changed back again, practise any form of magic against their captor. In other words, they must admit defeat.'

Miss Cackle looked embarrassed.

'Oh, yes!' she said brightly. 'I remember now. It slipped my mind for the moment. Did you hear that, Agatha? Do you think they can hear us, Miss Hardbroom?'

'Most certainly,' replied Miss Hardbroom. 'Perhaps you could line them up on your desk, and ask your sister to step forward?'

'What a splendid idea,' said Miss Cackle, who was beginning to enjoy herself. 'Help me, Mildred, my dear.'

They lined the snails up on the desk and Miss Cackle asked Agatha to step forward. One snail shuffled rather reluctantly out of line.

'Listen, Agatha,' said Miss Cackle.

'You must admit that you don't really have much choice. If you will agree to abide by the Witches' Code, then we can change you back, but not otherwise. If you agree, go back into line so that we know what you want us to do.'

The snail shuffled back into line again.

Miss Hardbroom spoke the words of the spell which released them, and suddenly the room was full of witches, all looking furious and talking angrily at the same time. The noise was terrible.

'Will you be quiet at once!' commanded Miss Cackle.

She turned to Mildred who was still perched on her chair. 'You may go back to bed, Mildred, and in view of what you have done for the school this morning, I think we will have to forget about the interview you were to have had with Miss Hardbroom and myself this afternoon. Don't you agree, Miss Hardbroom?'

Miss Hardbroom raised one eyebrow and Mildred's heart sank.

'Before I agree, Miss Cackle, if you'll forgive me,' she said, 'I would just like to ask Mildred what she was doing wandering about on the mountain when she should have been in bed?'

'I – I was out for a walk, Miss Hardbroom,' replied Mildred.

'And you just happened to have your spell book with you.'

'Yes,' agreed Mildred, unhappily.

'Such devotion to the school!' said Miss Hardbroom, smiling in a most unpleasant way. 'Taking your spell book with you wherever you go. I expect you were also singing the school song as you rambled along, weren't you, my dear?'

Mildred looked at the floor. She could feel all the other witches staring at her.

'I think we must let the child go to bed,'

said Miss Cackle. 'Run along now, Mildred.'

Mildred shot out of the room before her form-mistress could say anything else, and was in bed in five seconds!

CHAPTER TEN

AT noon the rising bell clanged through the corridors but Mildred pulled the pillow over her head and went back to sleep. It wasn't long before the door of her room burst open.

'Wake up, Mildred!' shrieked Maud, seizing the pillow and hitting her friend over the head with it.

Mildred screwed up her eyes against the daylight and saw what seemed to be hundreds of people around the bed all talking and shouting. Maud was actually *on* the bed, bouncing up and down.

'What's the matter?' asked Mildred, sleepily.

'As if you didn't know!' replied Maud, breathless from bouncing. 'The whole school's talking about it.'

'About what?' said Mildred, who was still half-asleep.

'*Will* you wake up?' shrieked Maud, pulling the bedclothes back. 'You saved the whole school from Miss Cackle's wicked sister, that's all!'

Mildred sat bolt upright.

'So I did!' she exclaimed, and everyone laughed.

'Miss Cackle's called a meeting in the Great Hall,' said Dawn and Gloria, two other members of Form One. 'You'd better hurry and dress, she'll expect you to be there.'

Mildred jumped out of bed and her friends went off to the hall. She was soon

ready and ran to join them, shoelaces
trailing along the floor as usual.

Maud had saved a place for her, and
Mildred was embarrassed to notice that
everyone stared as she came into the
hall. While they waited for the teachers to
arrive, Mildred decided to tell her friend
about Ethel.

'Listen,' she whispered, leaning towards Maud so that no one could hear.
'It wasn't my fault about the display.

Ethel cast a spell on the broomstick that she lent me, and I know because she told me. Don't tell anyone else, will you? But I wanted you to know because I don't want you thinking that I was just being clumsy.'

'But everyone already knows,' said Maud.

'Do they?' exclaimed Mildred. 'Who told them?'

'Well, you know what Ethel's like,' replied Maud. 'She just had to tell someone how clever she'd been so she told Harriet, and Harriet thought it was a dreadful thing to do so *she* told everyone else. No one's talking to Ethel now and Miss Hardbroom found out too and was furious with her.'

'Shhhhh!' said someone. 'They're coming.'

Everyone stood up as Miss Cackle came

in, followed by Miss Hardbroom and all
the other teachers.

'You may sit down, girls,' said the
headmistress. 'As you all know, the school
narrowly escaped invasion this morning.
Had it not been for a certain young
member of the school we should not be
here but would be hopping about turned
into frogs.'

The girls laughed.

'No, no, girls! Do not laugh! It would not be at all funny had it happened. However, as it did *not* happen, I proclaim the rest of today a half holiday in honour of Mildred Hubble. Mildred, would you come up here for a moment?'

Mildred went bright red and was pushed to her feet. She stumbled through the rows of chairs, tripping over feet as she went, and clumped across the platform to Miss Cackle's table.

'Now don't be shy, my dear,' said Miss Cackle beaming. She turned to the school. 'Come along, school! Three cheers for our heroine Mildred.'

Mildred blushed and twisted her fingers behind her back as the cheers rang out.

It was a relief to 'the heroine' when it was all over. As they filed out of the hall, she was thumped on the back and congratulated by everyone – except for Ethel who gave Mildred the nastiest look you've ever seen.

'Good old Mil!' yelled someone.

'We'll get out of our chanting test, thanks to you,' said someone else.

'Thanks for the holiday!'

'Thanks, Mil!' And so on.

Maud flung an arm around her friend.

'You did look embarrassed,' she said. 'You went ever so red, I could see you from the back of the hall!'

'Oh, *don't*,' said Mildred. 'Let's go and fetch the kittens and make the most of our holiday.'

'One moment,' said a chilling voice that they knew so well. The two girls turned to find their form-mistress standing behind them. They jumped to attention at once, wondering what they had done which was a natural reaction whenever Miss Hardbroom spoke.

This time, however, to their amazement, she smiled, a friendly smile not like the usual curl at the corner of the lips.

'I just wanted to say thank you, Mildred,' she said. 'Run along now, girls, and enjoy your holiday before it's over.'

She smiled again and vanished.

The girls just stared at each other.

'Sometimes,' said Mildred, 'I think she probably isn't as mean as we think she is.'

'Perhaps you are right, Mildred,' said

Miss Hardbroom's voice from behind Mildred's ear, and the two girls jumped in horror!

Mildred grabbed her friend's hand and they hurried away down the corridor out into the misty playground, leaving Miss Hardbroom's laughter echoing from nowhere along the empty passage.

If you have enjoyed

THE WORST WITCH

you might like to read the next book in the series,
in which Mildred finds herself in deep trouble again –
all because of the new girl, Enid Nightshade.

Read on to find out what happens!

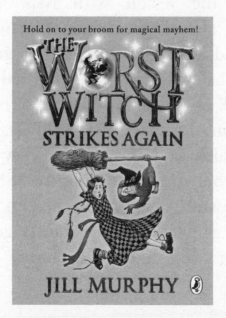

Hold on to your broom for magical mayhem!

THE WORST WITCH STRIKES AGAIN

JILL MURPHY

FTER Assembly the girls marched to the music-room for their chanting lesson with Miss Bat the chanting mistress. She was tiny, thin and very old with frizzy grey hair which she wore in a plait twisted around the back of her head. Because of her habit of pressing her jaw into her chest, she had three chins and this looked very odd on top of her thin little figure. She wore circular steel glasses attached to a chain round her neck (not the dainty gold kind but more like a bicycle chain) and she always had a conductor's baton tucked behind her ear.

She sat at the piano in a black dress with grey flowers and played a rousing march as the girls entered.

'Chanting's ever so dull,' whispered Mildred to Enid as they marched into the music-room.

'Don't you believe it,' Enid whispered back with a surprisingly wicked glint in her eye.

They all took their places, and Mildred managed to position herself with Maud on one side and Enid on the other, though Maud still looked very crotchety and wouldn't return Mildred's smile.

Miss Bat struck up the opening chord to a chant that they all knew very well, and the girls began.

To Mildred's surprise, Enid was singing completely out of tune – not loud enough for Miss Bat to hear, but loud enough so that Mildred couldn't concentrate on the right note herself. Verse after verse droned on with Enid just missing the correct note and the pupils around her struggling to keep in tune.

Mildred sneaked a look at Enid, who was smiling sweetly and obviously doing it on purpose, then glanced at Maud who was trying desperately to keep a straight face. A sudden mad burst of uncontrollable laughter welled up in Mildred. She clenched her teeth and racked her brains to think of something sad, but the sound of Enid's voice droning flatly on beside her was too much and a loud snorting noise erupted from Mildred's nose like a motorbike starting up.

Mildred put her hands across her mouth and even tried stuffing her handkerchief into it, but it was no use, a real fit of the giggles was upon her and she just doubled up with helpless laughter and giggled till her face ached.

'Mildred Hubble!' The inevitable words rang out across the room in a tone which implied that Miss Bat would stand no more nonsense. Everyone had stopped chanting, and Mildred's peals of laughter echoed embarrassingly round the silent walls.

'Come out here at once!' ordered Miss Bat.

Mildred clumped through the rows of

pupils and stood next to the piano. She took a deep breath and managed to look serious, though her face was flaming and the sound of Enid's voice still resounded in her head.

When Miss Bat was angry there were

two things she always did. First, her head would begin nodding (which it was doing now) and, secondly, she would take the baton from behind her ear and begin conducting an invisible orchestra (which she was also doing now). Mildred could tell that she was furious.

'What, may I ask, is so hilarious that you are prepared to disrupt the entire chanting lesson for the sake of it?' inquired Miss Bat coldly. 'No one else seems to be laughing. Perhaps you would let us all in on the joke!'

Mildred stole a glance at Maud and Enid. Maud was staring intently at her feet, and Enid was gazing at the ceiling, the picture of innocence.

'It was –' began Mildred, but a splutter of laughter came out and she dissolved into a giggling wreck again.

At last the wave subsided and she was left breathless, but able to speak.

'*Now*, Mildred,' quavered Miss Bat, in a

voice like a taut violin string, 'I'm waiting for a reasonable explanation.'

'Enid was singing out of tune,' said Mildred.

'Well!' said Miss Bat. 'I hardly think that is a reason for such a display of appalling manners. Come here, Enid my dear.'

Enid came and stood next to Mildred by the piano.

'Now, my dear,' said Miss Bat kindly, 'you must not feel shy because you can't sing very well. I hope you are not too upset just because Mildred decided to make a spectacle of herself on your account. Now, let me hear you sing one or two bars of "Eye of Toad" and we shall see if we can help you along a little.'

Enid obliged in the same wavering, off-key voice as before,

'Eye of toad,
Ear of bat,

Leg of frog,
Tail of cat.
Drop them in,
Stir it up,
Pour it in a silver cup.'

This was the last straw for Mildred, who abandoned all efforts at keeping control and gave herself up to complete hysteria.

As you may imagine, it was also the last straw for Miss Bat, and Mildred found herself on her way to the headmistress's office for the first time that term.

A new term, and Mildred is determined to
lose her reputation as the worst witch
Miss Cackle's Academy has ever seen –
but things get rapidly out of hand.

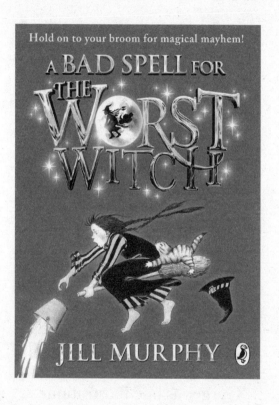

Millions of readers love Mildred Hubble –
and so will you . . .

puffin.co.uk

Mildred stows away her beloved cat, Tabby, on a class trip to the seaside. Trying to keep him out of sight of Miss Hardbroom leads her from one disaster to another, and soon she really is all at sea.

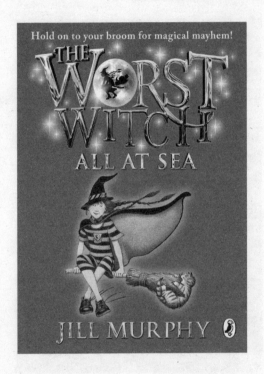

'Gorgeous line illustrations add to the charm' – *Lovereading4kids*

puffin.co.uk

A new teacher, a hair-growth spell gone
wrong and a cat who refuses to fly – can Mildred
overcome all obstacles and save the day?

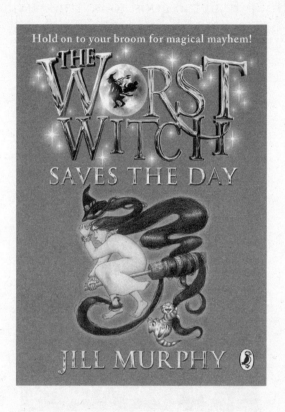

'A lovely, sparkly book' – *Observer*

puffin.co.uk

Mildred's done the best holiday project ever and she's sure Miss Hardbroom will be impressed. Even her arch-enemy, Ethel Hallow, is being friendly to her! But is it all too good to be true – will disaster strike again for the Worst Witch?

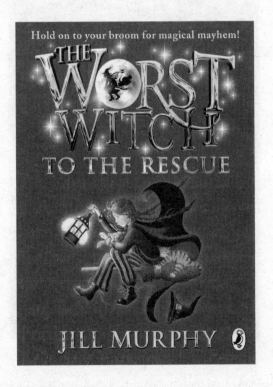

'Readers can't fail to warm to Mildred Hubble'
– *Booktrust*

puffin.co.uk

Winter Term starts surprisingly well for
Mildred Hubble. But when she sees a wishing star
things quickly take an unexpected turn.
Can she put things right or does this latest
disaster spell the end for the Worst Witch?

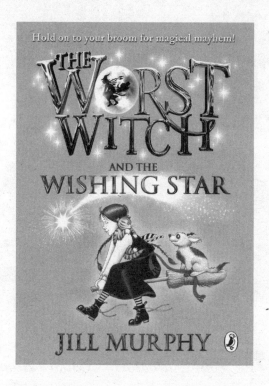

'Millions of young readers have fallen under the
spell of Jill Murphy's Worst Witch' – *Sunday Express*

puffin.co.uk

Get to know Mildred Hubble
from her very first disastrous day!

She may be the worst witch at Miss Cackle's Academy for Witches, but she's the best friend you could ever have.

puffin.co.uk

Your story starts here ...

Do you **love books** and
discovering new stories?
Then **www.puffin.co.uk**
is the place for you ...

• Thrilling adventures, fantastic fiction
and laugh-out-loud fun

• Brilliant videos featuring your favourite authors
and characters

• Exciting competitions, news, activities,
the Puffin blog and SO MUCH more ...

www.puffin.co.uk

It all started with a Scarecrow

Puffin is over seventy years old.
Sounds ancient, doesn't it? But Puffin has never been
so lively. We're always on the lookout for the next big
idea, which is how it began all those years ago.

Penguin Books was a big idea from the mind of
a man called Allen Lane, who in 1935 invented
the quality paperback and changed the world.
**And from great Penguins, great Puffins grew,
changing the face of children's books forever.**

The first four Puffin Picture Books were hatched in 1940 and the
first Puffin story book featured a man with broomstick arms called
Worzel Gummidge. In 1967 Kaye Webb, Puffin Editor, started the
Puffin Club, promising to **'make children into readers'**.
She kept that promise and over 200,000 children became devoted
Puffineers through their quarterly instalments of *Puffin Post*.

Many years from now, we hope you'll look back and
remember Puffin with a smile. **No matter what your age
or what you're into, there's a Puffin for everyone.**
The possibilities are endless, but one thing is for sure:
whether it's a picture book or a paperback, a sticker book
or a hardback, **if it's got that little Puffin
on it - it's bound to be good.**